Laura
and the
Great Quake

written and illustrated
by Jessica Clerk

**McGraw-Hill
School Division**

New York   Farmington

Laura Simonelli's fingers drummed as she waited to log on. Outside her window, the sunset was painting the city of Florence crimson and gold, but she barely noticed. Normally she appreciated the speed with which she could write from Italy to San Francisco. But not today. She punched in her cousin's address, and began to type, fingers flying over the keyboard.

Dear Celia,

Daniele did it AGAIN! I can't believe Mamma and Papa let him get away with this! There is no justice! He's never around when there are chores to do, but the minute the table's set and the food is served—like magic, he appears! He must have x-ray vision. Or the nose of a bloodhound.

After dinner, Mamma asked him to clear away and wash the dishes. So Daniele gives her this innocent look— well, of course he'd *love* to do the dishes, but his homework isn't finished.

Naturally, he didn't mention that the reason his homework wasn't done was that he had goofed off all afternoon playing soccer. So guess who got stuck doing his chores *after* dinner, too! I refuse to believe that Daniele is my *real* brother—he's got to be from some alien planet. Some *soccer-playing* alien planet!

Ciao, Laura

Dear Celia,

Victory! Justice is served! This afternoon, Papa stopped by the park and called Daniele out of his soccer game. At home, he made him do his homework right on the kitchen table, like he was still a *bambino* of four instead of fourteen. And then I got to watch TV, while Daniele had to vacuum, do the laundry, and then set the table.

And here's the best part—next week, when the plasterer is coming in, I get to go down to Assisi and spend a few days with Nonna, while Daniele has to stay and help out. Hooray! I love Nonna! I love Assisi!

I'll bring my laptop down and e-mail you every day. That way, it will almost be like you're there with me.

Ciao, Laura

Dear Celia,

I knew it was too good to be true. Mamma and Papa have changed their minds. Suddenly they remembered last year how Danielle helped the plumber pump out Nonna's basement, and they think he can help Nonna with other chores. So, he's going to Assisi, too. Poor Nonna. Poor me. Poor Assisi. Oh, well, at least he's not going INSTEAD of me.

Ciao, Laura

Dear Celia,

Thanks for writing so soon. No such luck—the pesky
nuisance is as healthy as Hercules—he sulked in the back
seat playing *Soccermania* all the way from Florence to
Assisi. Mamma talked about the history of Umbria on the
way—about the castles and the medieval fortresses. The
countryside looks so peaceful now—it's hard to believe that
armed knights rode into battle here.

Nonna was so happy to see us. You can't imagine the
feast that she laid out for us on the *terrazza.* Daniele
attacked the food like he'd been brought up by wolves.
Mamma told him to mind his manners, but Nonna couldn't
have been happier.

"I like it when the children eat," she said. Hah! She'll
change her tune when Wolf-boy eats her out of house and
home. The only time Daniele isn't thinking about soccer is
when he's thinking about food.

Tonight, after Mamma left, Nonna took us to the
movies. Then we went out for *gelato.* That's "ice cream" in
Italian—yum! Tomorrow, Nonna is taking us for a walk
around town, and then we're going to the basilica.

Ciao, Laura

Dear Celia,

What a terrific day! Nonna took us all over town—we walked along the old stone walls and towers. She's so spry that Daniele and I could barely keep up with her. We climbed up the Rocca—that's the fortress—and looked out over the battlements. It was just like being in the Middle Ages.

Nonna told us stories about Assisi's history—about the noble families and the *condottieri*—the warriors—who fought for control of this beautiful city. Listening to her, I almost thought I could see a regiment of knights galloping in the distance—their armor flashing in the sunlight. It was probably just sunlight glinting off a car somewhere.

The basilica looked rough and simple from the outside, but inside it was so beautiful. Light flooded through the stained glass windows and over Giotto's famous paintings of the life of San Francesco.

"The paintings are called *frescoes* because they were painted right on fresh plaster," Nonna said. She explained that the great painter and his assistants worked a little bit at a time, mixing only as much wet plaster as they could paint in a day.

I squinted because some of the paintings on the side walls were faded and hard to see. Then Nonna pointed out the paintings on the ceiling above the altar. The colors were still brilliant, even after seven hundred years! And you should have seen the ceiling of the vault! It was painted a deep blue, and sprinkled with gold stars.

"I'd love to paint that in my room," I said.

Nonna laughed. "I told Nonno—your grandfather—I'd like a ceiling just like that when we were first married. *Povero Nonno!* He tried three times but the farthest he got was a big blob of blue paint on the middle of the ceiling. Finally he confessed that he got dizzy just standing on a step stool."

She pointed to the ceiling. "It's a good thing he wasn't born in the thirteenth century. If he was working for Giotto he would have had to climb up and down sixty feet of scaffolding every day!"

I could have stayed there for hours, but Wolf-boy's stomach started rumbling. Nonna took us to a pizzeria nearby for lunch. I wish I had my watercolors with me; I would have loved to sketch the cathedral. At least I got to pick up a book and some great postcards at the entrance.

As we waited for pizza, Nonna turned to Daniele. "So, what do you think of the basilica?" she asked.

"Well. . . it's big enough to play soccer in," Daniele said finally. A tour guide behind us burst out laughing. I was so embarrassed I wanted to crawl under a pew!

I really wish you were here, Celia. If you come to Italy next summer, maybe we can come visit Nonna together. I know you'd like her. And I know you'd love Assisi. In the meantime, I'm starting a postcard collection. I'll send you the ones I like best.

Ciao, Laura

Dear Celia,

Nonna was tired after our long walk, so Daniele and I took her home to rest. Then we wandered around on our own. We went back to that *gelateria*—they had the best chocolate ice cream! As we munched away, an old man led his horse across the *piazza.* He was pulling a cart of the most beautiful flowers!

Before I could say a word, Daniele ran over. The *fioraio* held the horse's reins while Daniele picked flowers out of the buckets. "I'll take some of these," he said, "and these, and these."

The *fioraio* saw me looking at the big brown horse. "*Signorina*, would you like to pet Cesare?" he asked. Cesare looked friendly under his big straw hat, so I patted his muzzle.

Then Daniele turned to me. "You're the artist in the family," he said. "Will you help me arrange them?" He made me sign the card with him, even though I didn't have any money to pay for half the flowers.

"These are from me and Laura," Daniele said, presenting Nonna with the huge bouquet and adding, "for our favorite grandmother." Nonna loved them—she gave us both a huge hug.

It's an eerie thought, Celia, but sometimes I think my brother might be human after all.

Ciao, Laura

Dear Celia,

You'll never believe what happened! Well, maybe you will, because it's been all over the news the last few days! I've just been too busy and too spooked out to write to you.

Our last night in Assisi, Daniele and I were sleeping in the guest room. Suddenly, in the middle of the night, I was jerked awake—I felt the bed move—for an instant I lay still trying to figure out if I was still dreaming. . . and then the mirror fell and crashed on the floor.

In a second, Nonna was in the room. "Laura! Daniele! Grab your clothes and come outside, quickly!"

"Nonna, what is it?"

"*Il terremoto*—the earthquake!"

9

The floor shook again—we lunged at our things, and raced downstairs. Outside, in the piazza, Daniele pulled on his jeans—and I pulled my overalls on top of my pajamas. I looked at my watch—it was nearly three o'clock in the morning.

Soon, Nonna's neighbors spilled out onto the street. Some were fully dressed and some just wore bathrobes; everyone looked stunned.

Nonna knew all of them. Nervously, people looked up at the old houses. Roof tiles were in the streets—we could see cracked windows. Pots of geraniums had tumbled from windowsills, smashing onto the ground.

We stepped over them as we walked around, trying to keep warm. We were lucky that it was only late September— it would have been awful out there in some January squall! When you're only wearing jeans and a T-shirt at night, it can get pretty cold. One of Nonna's neighbors noticed we were shivering and offered us blankets.

For an earthquake, I guess it wasn't too bad after all, but it was still really scary. Daniele was scared, too, although he acted like he wasn't. He couldn't fool me. At least he didn't talk about soccer for once.

Finally, when it got light, Nonna let us go back inside. But she insisted that we pull the mattresses down and sleep under the heavy wooden beds so we had some protection in case there were aftershocks.

It was weird—like camping out in your own home. I was just falling asleep when I remembered my laptop. I crawled out and dragged that under the bed too, just in case.

In the morning we looked over the damage. It didn't seem too bad—broken mirrors, pictures knocked down, cracked plates. Nonna got upset when she saw the bouquet of flowers on the floor in a puddle of water and smashed glass.

"Well, it could have been much worse," Nonna sighed. Then out on the terrace, she saw the big crack that ran up the wall and shook her head. "I don't like the look of that, but I guess it can be fixed."

Daniele volunteered to go out to the corner café to bring back some *caffe-latte* and pastries while I swept up the broken roof tiles out on the terrace.

Just as we sat down to eat, the phone rang. Our parents had heard the news reports. They were practically hysterical. "Yes, yes, I'm fine, the *bambini* are safe, everything's fine," Nonna said, but Mamma and Papa wouldn't believe her till they talked to us. "We're driving down immediately," Mamma said. "And tell Nonna to take it easy till we get there!"

Hah! Believe me, Celia, our Nonna is a pretty stubborn lady. Nobody tells her anything! Daniele and I begged her to sit down, and let us take care of the mess. She was obviously tired, but she refused. For once, I *actually* saw my brother racing around with a mop and broom! Well, at least we managed to get most of the cleaning done before Nonna could get to it.

Daniele and I were both relieved when Mamma and Papa rushed in. They must have set some kind of speed record, to make it by eleven. Just as Nonna was protesting that everything was all right, we felt a tremor. A few minutes later, the second earthquake struck.

I'll tell you more later.

Ciao, Laura

P.S. I'm glad you liked the post cards I sent.

Dear Celia,

I'm sorry I couldn't write you the last few days. Things have been really crazy lately. Anyway, I'm sure you heard about the second quake. That was the one that damaged the basilica—and the frescoes by Giotto.

People were inside trying to estimate the damage from the first earthquake when the second big shock hit. Part of the ceiling vault crashed down. Several people died—it was really horrible!

It's hard to believe that we had been there just a day or two earlier. From a distance we saw the ambulances in the square; rescue workers huddled together—I guess we should all be grateful that more people weren't hurt.

Some villages closer to the center of the quake were nearly destroyed—I heard that the shocks were felt as far away as Rome. That's nearly one hundred kilometers away!

Now for our big news. Nonna is coming to live with us! The second shock damaged the foundations of her house badly. Papa's engineer said it was unsafe.

At first, she refused to move. "I insist on staying in my own home!" she said. "We Umbrians have lived through plagues, famines, and wars. We can live through earthquakes, too." Mamma and Papa argued for hours; they were at their wit's end, but Nonna wouldn't budge.

Daniele and I listened from the other room. We didn't have to eavesdrop—everyone was yelling so loud you could have heard them from a block away!

Then Daniele winked at me. "Why don't *we* ask her? I'll tell her that Mamma's not feeding us enough," he joked. Well, believe it or not, it worked!

We waited till our parents went out; and then we asked her. When they came back Nonna announced that she *would* move to Florence—but only to help look after her *nipoti*!

We're going home with Mamma by bus. Papa is going to stay in Assisi for a while to help Nonna pack up her things and make arrangements to stabilize the house. After all, we don't want it crashing down into the street!

Meanwhile, Daniele is giving up his big bedroom and moving into the smaller room, so Nonna can bring up as many of her things as possible. And let me tell you, his room is a real mess. I'm helping him take down his soccer posters. The walls are covered with them—he's even got them on the ceiling.

I'd better get back to work, Celia. So glad you got a puppy. I'll write more later.

Ciao, Laura

Dear Celia,

Daniele and I talked to Nonna on the phone today. She was putting a brave face on things, but we could tell that she was really sad about moving and leaving her home.

"Florence is a beautiful city, but I've lived in Assisi all my life. Still," she said, "I guess change is good for you. It will keep me young, like my *nipoti*."

Mamma said Nonna was sad about leaving many of her friends behind. She was also sad about the wreckage in the cathedral—no one knows how long it will take to restore the frescoes. Or, if they *can* be restored at all. I hope they can be, but I'm sure it's going to take a long time.

Ciao, Laura

Dear Celia,

Daniele and I were trying to figure out how to cheer Nonna up when she moves in with us. He suggested putting some flowers in her room, but I said it would take more than a bunch of flowers to cheer her up.

Then I got the best idea! I'd been looking at the books and postcards I brought back from Assisi. I was remembering what a good time we had there. Then I had a brainstorm!

Guess what, Celia—we're going to paint Nonna the ceiling she always wanted! Deep blue, and spangled with gold stars— just like the one in the Basilica.

Daniele says he's going to follow my instructions. After all, I *am* the artist in the family. Or so he tells me. Well, this artist is off to the store. We're going to buy gold and blue paint, and some brushes, and then we've got a lot of work to do.

If it comes out OK, I'll send you a photograph. Maybe I'll get Daniele to sign it, too. He may be a soccer-playing alien, but he's not such a bad brother.

Ciao, Laura